The gleeks

Contents

Chapter 1 Adam the gardener

Professor Quickly was as pleased as a dog with two tails. He'd just opened a letter which told him he'd been left a fortune by an old uncle of his who had passed away. He had to tell somebody, so he rushed across to the little house in the woods.

Adam and Polly Hardwick were just as pleased as the Professor when he told them what had happened.

'I can pay all the bills!' shouted the Professor, 'and there'll be plenty left to make this the best Animal Park that anyone has ever seen!'

He looked around the grounds. 'Adam, I need a Chief Gardener, and now I can afford to pay you I'd like you to have the job!'

Adam didn't even stop to think. 'I'd love to do it,' he said. 'These grounds need a lot of work. There are weeds shooting up all over the drive, the flower beds are a mess, and lots of trees are ready to fall down.'

'I must spend some time making proper plans,' said the Professor. 'All the animals I collected can stop at the zoo for the moment. We must do everything properly. We need animal shelters and places for storing food. Then we'll have to put in tracks and trails and picnic spots for all our visitors. And I want to build a big, glass tropical house for all the exotic plants I collected. This needs a lot of thinking about. It will take months to do everything properly, but first I must draw up some plans. I can't wait to get started!'

And leaving Adam and Polly standing there, the Professor rushed back to his study to begin work.

Polly and Adam hardly saw him for the next two months!

While the Professor was working hard in his study, Adam began the difficult job of sorting out the garden.

Until the Professor had moved in, Crack Puzzle House had been empty for years, and the garden had been allowed to get into a very bad state.

Adam worked very hard, and Tom and Kate often helped him, but it was an impossible job. There was far too much to do.

The grounds of Crack Puzzle House were very big indeed. Some parts of the grounds were so thick with weeds, thorns and brambles that it was impossible to move.

But what Tom and the children didn't know was that they were about to get some unexpected help. The gleeks had finished their tunnels, and they were ready to begin work.

Adam, Tom and Kate were being watched!

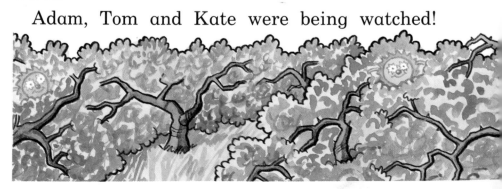

Chapter 2 All about gleeks

Gleeks are very timid, and they do not like to be seen. They are very clever at making sure that nobody ever spots them.

The gleeks have several ways of becoming invisible. Their first trick is to stand perfectly still – it is astonishing how many times this works. Adults and children simply go past them without even seeing them.

Another trick they use is to pull in their arms and turn around. Now they look just like a little bush.

But the last trick is the best of all. Gleeks can become a different colour. So if a gleek is standing in front of a brick it will become a reddish-brown. If a gleek is standing next to some bright flowers it can match their colours. And even more astonishing, if a gleek is standing in front of something which has a lot of colours, its skin can become mottled so that it looks just the same as the background.

So it is no wonder that it was a very long time before anyone was able to spot them!

Each week the gleeks visited every living thing in the garden. Whenever they found a plant that needed help they spent some time with it. They mended broken branches and stems, they watered plants that had become dry, and they collected seeds and bulbs and planted them out in different parts of the garden.

They knew where every animal family lived, and they often visited them. And there were lots of animals to visit!

On the lake there were ducks and coots. Sand martins nested in the banks of the lake, swifts darted across the water hunting for insects, and kingfishers hunted for the shoals of fish.

In the trees there were thousands of insects and woodpeckers, blackbirds, thrushes, jackdaws, rooks and owls. Squirrels lived there too.

Under the trees there were voles, rabbits, foxes, moles, stoats, weasels and grass snakes. There were ants' nests, slugs, snails and spiders.

The gleeks knew all these animals, and made sure that they did not harm the trees and plants.

When they found animals that were hurting their plants, such as a snail eating green leaves and shoots, they did not kill it. They simply moved it to a patch of weeds, so that it could carry on eating and get rid of the weeds at the same time.

The only animal the gleeks did not know about was the Litterbug, who was still on his travels. Unluckily, even though the gleeks visited every part of the garden, they did not spot the Litterbug's cave. If they had, it would have saved them a lot of bother later on!

Every gleek had a set of home-made tools. They had spades, forks, trowels, rakes, dibbers and snippers.

They kept these tools in a little wicker basket called a trug. At the end of each day they cleaned the tools and stacked them away properly in the 'gardening room' which was inside their den.

Even though the gleeks worked hard, and never lazed about, they looked forward to playing at the end of the day.

Every evening, as the sun was going down, they crept out to a quiet part of the garden to have some fun and games. They loved to run about, to play tag and leapfrog and to tumble around. Even though they worked hard all day, they were still wide awake and full of beans!

The gleeks loved to play practical
jokes. They jumped out from behind bushes and
rocks. They dropped things on each other.
They set little traps for each other with
bits of string and rope.

They played tricks on some of the animals
in the garden too. They crept up on them and
shouted 'Boo!'

Then, at the end of the day, they went
back into their tunnel for a well-deserved
night's sleep.

Chapter 3 Tom and Kate build a hide

As the days passed by, the garden began to bloom. Trees which had been ready to fall down were now looking strong and green, all the weeds were vanishing, and flowers were sprouting up all over the place.

It was not too long before Adam began to suspect that someone else, or something else, was working in the garden.

Every morning, as he wandered round the garden with Tom and Kate, thinking about which job he was going to do next, there would be something different to see. A patch of weeds would have gone and fresh flowers planted in their place, or a rotten tree branch would have vanished, or a tangled pile of brambles would have been cut down and taken away.

Adam couldn't understand it.

'Have you been coming into the garden and working when I'm not looking?' he asked Tom and Kate, but they shook their heads. They were as puzzled as he was.

'Go on with you,' said Dad. 'You're kidding me! I know you've been sneaking out and doing some extra gardening, and I want you to know that I'm very pleased with you. Come on, you can help me to cut the grass.'

Tom and Kate looked at each other. 'Can we just play today, Dad? You can cut the grass by yourself, can't you?'

Adam was surprised. Normally the two children wanted to help him with every job. But he was glad that they wanted to play for a while. They deserved a rest.

'Play as long as you want,' he said. 'You know where I'll be if you need me,' and he went off to start up the grass-cutter.

As soon as their dad had gone, Tom and Kate grinned at each other.

'Time to get on with our plan,' said Tom.

'Yes,' answered Kate. 'Crack Puzzle House has given us another puzzle to crack.'

The two children did not intend to play at all. They were going to track down the gleeks!

When their dad had gone, Tom and Kate got ready for the hunt. For several days now they had been sure that something was watching them. They kept seeing things out of the corner of their eyes, but when they turned round there was nothing there.

Last night, whispering together in Tom's bedroom, they had worked out exactly what to do. Kate had come up with the best plan.

'We must think about how bird-watchers get close to birds,' she had said. 'They build a hide, then they sit quietly inside and wait to see what happens. That's what we must do.' Tom agreed at once. He thought it was a brilliant plan.

The two children found an open patch of grass in the trees and set to work to build their hide. As soon as it was finished they crept inside. Tom had found his old telescope, and they took it in turns to watch the ground all around them.

The children sat there until nearly tea-time, but all they saw were rabbits and birds.

Tom was fed up. He was cramped and hungry.

'Let's go home,' he whispered. 'I want something to eat.'

'Just five more minutes,' whispered Kate. 'Please!'

In the end they stayed there for another twenty minutes. Now it was Tom's turn to look through the telescope and Kate was getting bored. She was just about to agree to go home when Tom hissed,

'There's something moving in the bushes!'

The two children stopped breathing and kept quite still, as a little troop of very odd animals crept out.

The children didn't know it, but they had chosen the spot where the gleeks came to play every night. They watched in amazement as the gleeks began to chase each other.

'We've got to try to make friends with them,' whispered Kate.

'How?' whispered Tom.

But just then, there was a loud shout from the woods,

'Tom! Kate! Where are you?'
And in less time than it takes to blink an eye, the gleeks vanished!

Dad had come to call them in for tea, and he had frightened the gleeks away before Tom and Kate could even try to make friends with them.

'What have you been up to today?' asked Dad, looking at the hide and the telescope. Tom and Kate went red. They didn't know what to say.

'I know just what you've been doing,' said Dad, 'you've been bird-watching. Well done! Now come home and get your tea before it goes cold.'

As soon as they had finished their tea, the two children crept up to Tom's bedroom to discuss what to do next.

'If only Dad hadn't come along just then,' groaned Tom, 'we may have been able to make friends with them!'

'I don't think so,' said Kate. 'I think they would have run away. We must find something to tempt them.'

'That's good,' said Tom. 'I wonder what they like to eat?'

Chapter 4 Greedy gleeks

The two children rushed down to see Mum.

'Mum,' said Kate, 'today we played in the woods all day, and we want to go back in the morning. Can we take a picnic with us?'

'Yes,' said Mum. 'Go into the pantry and get what you want.'

Before long, Kate and Tom had filled a carrier bag with all sorts of things to eat. The bag looked as if it was ready to burst.

'My goodness,' said Mum when she saw how full it was. 'Are you sure you've got enough?'

'Just about,' smiled Tom. 'We got quite hungry today, didn't we Kate?'
Kate nodded, then the two children went up

to bed. They couldn't wait for morning!

The next day, Kate and Tom were back in the woods. They were sorting out all the food from the carrier bag.

They had forgotten to bring plates with them, so they had picked up some big, flat leaves to use.

Soon there was a trail of leaves leading from the middle of the clearing, right up to the hide. Each leaf was piled up with good things to eat.

The children had set out lots of different food. There was Marmite, cornflakes, crisps, shortcake, yoghurt, a lump of cheese, beetroot, cold baked beans, three jars of strawberry jam and two jars of orange marmalade. They must have taken everything from the pantry!

The children sat inside the hide and waited for something to happen. They did not have to wait long. In less than ten minutes the little animals were back again. The children's plan had worked.

The children watched in amazement as the little creatures set about the food. They ate absolutely everything. As they finished one pile, they went on to the next, getting closer and closer to the hide where Tom and Kate were sitting.

As they reached the hide, it was plain to see that the jam and marmalade were a big hit. The gleeks loved it.

Very quietly, Tom and Kate crept out.
'Good morning,' said Kate quietly.

The gleeks scattered. But one unlucky
gleek had a jar of jam stuck to his head. He
couldn't see where he was going. He just ran
round and round and round.

In the end, he collapsed on the ground. Kate bent down and picked him up. Making sure not to hurt him, she pulled the sticky jam jar from his head.

'Don't be frightened,' she whispered. 'We won't hurt you. We want to be friends.'

She put him down on the ground.

'Go and tell the rest of them. We just want to get to know you. We'll wait here.' The gleek blinked, smiled at them, and shot off into the trees as fast as his little legs would carry him.

'That won't work,' muttered Tom. 'We won't see him again.'

But in the end Tom had to admit that Kate was right. Two minutes later, the little family of gleeks trooped back across the clearing, came right up to Tom and Kate then sat down on the grass. They were all blinking rapidly, and they looked ready to run at any minute. Very slowly, Tom and Kate sat down next to them.

'Right!' said Kate. 'Here goes. I've
never seen anything like you in my life.
Where do you come from?' and then she
giggled.

'Silly me!' she said. 'They can't speak.
They won't understand a word I'm saying!'

'Yes we can!' squeaked the gleeks.

For the next three hours Kate, Tom and the gleeks chatted away happily. The gleeks told the children about their home in Brazil, and how their job in life was to look after all living things. They explained that adults were often to blame for harming living things. Adults polluted the rivers and the seas, cut down forests and built dirty chimneys which blotted out the sky with thick, black smoke.

'We try to put things right,' said one of the gleeks, 'but it's a very difficult job.'

'Yes,' said another. 'It's a shame, because children like you are good to living things, but when children become adults they seem to forget. Then they add to the mess!'

'We hide from adults,' said the first gleek. 'We only make friends with children. You must not tell any adults about us or they will try to hunt us down and catch us, and we will have to go away.'

'Our dad won't hunt you down,' said Tom. 'He loves living things, that's why he's a gardener!'

'We know that,' said the gleek, 'and we are trying to help him. But we think it will be safer if you don't tell him about us. Will you give us your word not to tell anyone else about us?' The children nodded.

'Good!' said the gleeks. 'Now come along with us and we'll let you see where we live.'

Soon the children were standing in the middle of the maze.

'This is it!' said the gleeks.

The children were puzzled. All they could see was the fountain.

Then the gleeks opened the hidden door, and the children could see the dark tunnel leading downwards.

'What a clever doorway!' said Kate. 'No-one could ever tell it was there!'

'We must go now,' said the gleeks, 'but you can come and visit us again. Just make sure that no-one else sees you.'

'We will!' said the children, as they trotted home for their tea.

Chapter 5 Bulldozer!

Several more weeks passed. The children often visited the gleeks, and at last Professor Quickly finished his plans.

One bright morning he called on Adam Hardwick and his family and told them to be ready for one or two surprises.

'Things are going to start happening from today onwards,' said the Professor. 'There will be a lot of workmen about the place, and there may be a bit of mess at first, but it will all be cleaned up in the end. When everything's finished, I'll send for all the animals from the zoo, and then we can have our Grand Opening Day!'

And just as the Professor had finished speaking, there was a loud rumble, and a line of heavy trucks came chugging up the drive.

Suddenly, the garden was filled with big men in hard yellow hats, starting up bulldozers and dumper trucks, unloading piles of pipes, stacks of bricks, heaps of sand and bundles of wood.

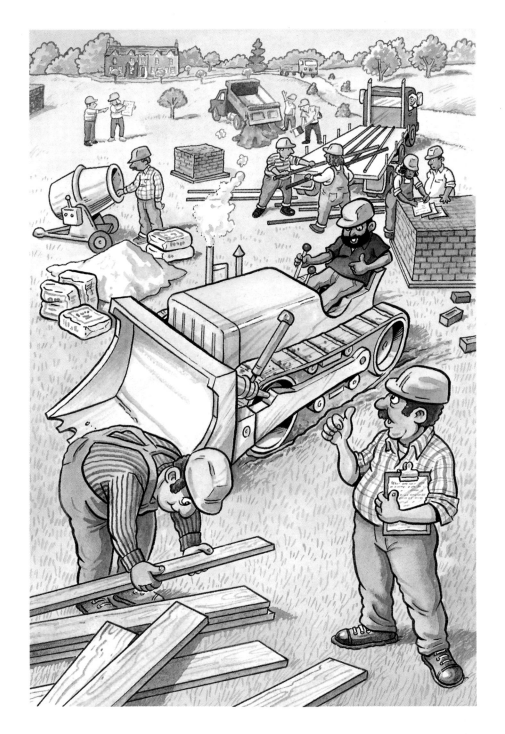

Adam, Polly, Tom and Kate goggled in amazement. They had never seen anything like it! Professor Quickly rubbed his hands together, and waved at one of the biggest men.

'Right you are!' he shouted. 'Get on with it!'

The man nodded. He climbed into a big bulldozer and started it up. And then something terrible happened. The big man lowered the big steel blade of the bulldozer and drove at the maze.

'Stop!' shouted Kate, but she was too late. There was a loud cracking and splitting sound as the bushes from the maze were flattened and uprooted.

Tom and Kate ran towards the bulldozer, trying to stop it, but Adam caught them just in time. He was pale and trembling. They had nearly run under the big metal tracks.

'What are you trying to do?' he asked them. 'You could have been killed!'

Before long, the maze had gone. Even the fountain had been smashed to bits, and the broken, splintered bushes were being loaded onto the backs of trucks to be carted away.

'It had to go,' said the Professor sadly. 'We couldn't have little children getting lost in a maze on our Grand Opening Day!' Nobody could understand why Tom and Kate were sobbing and crying.

As soon as all the men had packed up for the day, Tom and Kate rushed around the grounds looking for the gleeks. When it got dark they dashed home for their torches and went on with their hunt.

But it was no good. There was not a gleek to be seen anywhere.

'They must have been trapped in their tunnels,' sobbed Kate, 'and we were too late to save them!'

At last they had to give up. It was useless. The gleeks must have been killed. The two children felt that they had lost their best friends.

Over the next two months, lots of interesting things were happening in the garden, but the two children would not even go out. They were pale and sad-looking and Adam and Polly often heard them crying in the middle of the night. Polly went to see the Professor.

'Hang on until the Park is finished,' he said. 'I think I may be able to help.'

Chapter 6 Tom and Kate go out

At last the day came when all the workmen left. The Professor didn't wait. He marched down to the little house in the woods and insisted on seeing the two children.

He was shocked to see how thin and pale they were, but he pretended that everything was normal.

'I need your help,' he told them. 'Everything is finished and I've sent for the animals. They'll be here in less than a week, and I need you to help them settle in.'

The two children perked up. Nothing could take the place of the gleeks, but perhaps animals from far off lands would help them to forget. For the first time in weeks, there was a sparkle in their eyes.

'Come on,' said the Professor. 'You haven't seen all the things the workmen have done. You must come and look.'

He took the children outside. They gasped in astonishment. The garden had been transformed!

'Wow!' shouted Tom. 'This is fantastic!'

Kate turned to the Professor. There was a lump in her throat.

'What's inside that big glass dome where the maze used to be?' she asked.

'That's a Tropical House,' answered the Professor. 'It's full of the exotic and tropical plants I collected in Brazil. And there's even a pool in there. It looks wonderful. Why don't you and Tom go across and have a good look?'

'Can we?' gasped Tom.

'Go ahead,' said the Professor. 'I think you'll like it.'

The two children held hands and went slowly towards the big glass building. Perhaps this would help them to forget the gleeks.